KIDS' SPORTS STORIES

FREE THROW CONTEST

by Shawn Pyror

illustrated by Alex Patrick

PICTURE WINDOW BOOKS
a capstone imprint

Published by Picture Window Books,
an imprint of Capstone
1710 Roe Crest Drive, North Mankato, Minnesota 56003
capstonepub.com

Library of Congress Cataloging-in-Publication Data
Names: Pryor, Shawn, author. | Patrick, Alex, illustrator.
Title: Free throw contest / by Shawn Pryor ; illustrated by Alex Patrick.
Description: North Mankato, Minnesota : Picture Window Books, an imprint of Capstone, [2022] | Series: Kids' sports stories | Audience: Ages 5-7. | Audience: Grades K-1. | Summary: Donovan wants to enter the free throw contest at his school, but he worries that others will make fun of his unique way of shooting the ball.
Identifiers: LCCN 2021004258 (print) | LCCN 2021004259 (ebook) | ISBN 9781663909343 (hardcover) | ISBN 9781663921215 (paperback) | ISBN 9781663909312 (ebook pdf) |
Subjects: CYAC: Basketball—Fiction. | Contests—Fiction.
Classification: LCC PZ7.1.P7855 Fr 2022 (print) | LCC PZ7.1.P7855 (ebook) | DDC [E]—dc23
LC record available at https://lccn.loc.gov/2021004258
LC ebook record available at https://lccn.loc.gov/202100425

Designer: Tracy Davies

Printed and bound in the USA. 4270

TABLE OF CONTENTS

Glossary

 **backboard**–the large board behind a basketball hoop

 **free throw**–a shot in basketball made from behind the free throw line

 **line**–the free throw line is usually 15 feet from the basketball hoop

 **rim**–the circular part of a basketball hoop to which the net attaches

 **swish**–to make a shot in which the basketball falls through the rim without touching it

Chapter 1
TAKING A CHANCE

Donovan dashed toward the school's front doors with his friends. The school day was finally done! Then something caught his eye on the wall. It was a colorful sign for a **free throw** contest. The winner would get front-row seats to a pro basketball game!

"Wow!" said Donovan. "It would be awesome to see a pro basketball game."

"Sign up, Donovan!" Keisha said.

"Do it!" Billy said.

"I don't know. I like basketball, but I'm not *that* good at it," said Donovan.

"It can't hurt to try," Keisha said.

Some members of the basketball team walked by Donovan and his friends.

"There's no way you can win, Donovan. I'm the best free throw shooter in the whole school!" Nevin said.

"Yeah, you don't stand a chance!" said Jacob, one of Nevin's teammates.

"You can't tell me what I can't do, Nevin," Donovan said. "I'm going to sign up."

"Awesome! Show them what you can do!" Billy said.

"Good luck, Donovan. You're going to need it!" Nevin said. He smirked and walked away.

Chapter 2
PRACTICE

At home, Donovan practiced his free throws.

He shot the ball. The basketball fell short of the net.

I'll shoot harder on my next try, Donovan thought.

Donovan shot the ball with force. It clanged against the **rim** and bounced back at him. Donovan ducked to keep the ball from hitting him.

That was a little too hard. Maybe Nevin is right. I'm not good enough, Donovan thought.

Donovan's mom came outside. She saw the sad look on his face.

"What's wrong?" Mom asked.

"I signed up for a free throw contest, but I can't make a shot," Donovan said.

"Let me see how you shoot free throws," Mom said.

Donovan's free throws were too short
or too strong. Some bounced off the
backboard.

"How about shooting differently?" Mom
said. "Pass me the ball."

Donovan's mom shot her free throw.
Instead of shooting the regular way, she
shot underhanded with both hands!
Every shot **swished** through the hoop!

"Whoa! You're awesome, Mom!"
Donovan said. "Let me try!"

Donovan took the ball. With both hands under it, he took a shot. It went in!

He kept shooting this way, and nearly every shot went through the hoop.

"I'm doing it! I can make free throws now!" Donovan shouted.

Donovan was so happy, but suddenly he became sad.

"What if kids make fun of me for the way I shoot?" Donavan said.

"Then those kids aren't your friends,"
Mom said. "Just do your best. That's all
that matters. Don't worry about what
others think of you."

Chapter 3
THE CONTEST

It was the day of the contest. Donovan warmed up as his friends watched.

"I like your shooting style!" Keisha said.

"Thanks!" Donovan said.

Nevin saw Donovan shooting.

"That's so weird!" Nevin said.

The free throw contest started. Donovan felt everyone watching him as he walked to the line. His hands were sweaty. But when he took his first shot, the ball swished through the net!

Donovan made all his free throws. He was going to the next round! He smiled and waved to his friends.

Nevin and two other kids also made it to the second round. In round two, kids had one minute to make as many free throws as possible. The top two would go to the final round.

In round two, Donovan missed his first shot. But then he got on a roll. He made basket after basket. When the timer hit zero, Donovan was in second place! He was going to the final round against Nevin!

Nevin rolled his eyes. "You shoot free throws like a grandma," Nevin said. "You were lucky to get this far."

"Make fun of me all you want. It won't change how I shoot," Donovan said.

In the final round, Nevin went first.
He had to make as many free throws as
possible until he missed. After a while,
Nevin finally missed. He had made
thirteen free throws in a row.

For Donovan to win, he'd have to make fourteen free throws in a row, with no misses. He stepped to the free throw line and took a deep breath.

I can do this, he thought.

Donovan began shooting. Swish! He
kept going. Five. Ten. Thirteen! He had tied
Nevin! One more, and he would win!

Donovan's arms felt like rubber bands. He shot his last free throw and held his breath.

The ball rolled around the rim. It went through the net! Donovan won!

"I did it!" Donovan screamed. His friends joined him to celebrate.

Nevin walked up to Donovan. "Sorry I made fun of you for how you shoot. I was being a poor sport. You're really good!"

"Thanks!" Donovan said. "You want to go to the basketball game with me and my friends?"

"That would be awesome!" Nevin said.

PLAY H-O-R-S-E

Have fun while building your shooting skills with this basketball game.

What You Need:
- at least one friend
- a basketball
- a basketball hoop

What You Do:
- Decide who will go first.
- The first player chooses how to take a shot and the shot location.
- If the first player makes the shot, the other players have to do the exact same thing. If one of these players misses, they get a letter. The first letter is H.
- Once everyone has tried the first player's shot, the second player makes up a shot. The other players who miss must take a letter. If it's their first miss, they take an H. If it's their second miss, they take an O, and so on.
- Everyone keeps playing until someone misses enough times to spell the word HORSE. This person is out of the game.
- The one who's still in the game after everyone else has spelled HORSE is the winner!

REPLAY IT

Take another look at this illustration. How do you think Donovan felt when the basketball team members told him he wouldn't win? How would you feel if this happened to you?

Pretend you are Donovan. Write a letter to Nevin explaining how happy you were after he apologized and congratulated you for your win. Tell him how excited you are to go to the pro game.

ABOUT THE AUTHOR

Shawn Pryor is the creator and co-author of the graphic novel mystery series Cash and Carrie, co-creator and author of the 2019 GLYPH-nominated football/drama series Force, and author of *Kentucky Kaiju* and *Jake Maddox: Diamond Double Play*. In his free time, he enjoys reading, cooking, listening to streaming music playlists, and talking about why Zack from the Mighty Morphin Power Rangers is the greatest super hero of all time.

ABOUT
THE ILLUSTRATOR

Alex Patrick was born in the Kentish town of Dartford in the southeast of England. He has been drawing for as long as he can remember. His life-long love for cartoons, picture books, and comics has shaped him into the passionate children's illustrator he is today. Alex loves creating original characters. He brings an element of fun and humor to each of his illustrations and is often found laughing to himself as he draws.